MEET CYRUS AVERY, FATHER OF ROUTE 66

The Dreamer who Brought the World to His Town

First Printing, 2025

Illustrations and book design by Bailey Vidler
www.baileyvidler.com

ISBN 979-8-9988277-6-1 (hardcover)
ISBN 979-8-9988277-7-8 (paperback)
ISBN 979-8-9988277-8-5 (ebook)

To the Spirit of Rt. 66 and all
who paved the way — A.L.M.

For Grandma and Papa — B.V.

Visit us at **www.annettemurraybooks.com**

MEET CYRUS AVERY, FATHER OF ROUTE 66

The Dreamer who Brought the World to His Town

Written by Annette LaFortune Murray

Illustrated by Bailey Vidler

Travel in the 1900's in America was simple.

However, in 1921 the jangling ring of Cyrus Avery's telephone brought his highway planning meeting to a halt and signaled that change was coming.

"Hello, Cyrus Avery speaking. What can I help you with?" Cyrus asked.

On the other end of the line, an automobile factory manager explained, "New automobiles are rolling out of the factories in the East so fast there are NOT enough roads. Can you build more roads for all these new automobiles?"

"I believe we can!" Cyrus replied.

He believed a new highway could connect travelers across the country from Chicago to Santa Monica. He had no idea that the new highway would change tourism in America forever.

Before Cyrus began building roads, he designed a concrete, span bridge in 1916 across the Arkansas River in Tulsa, Oklahoma.

The new span bridge was perfect for carrying bicycles,
wagons, and small automobiles across the Arkansas River.
Many said Cyrus' team couldn't build it, but they did.

Cyrus got to work right away and called his highway team together to explore all the trails and paths west of the Mississippi River.

Most existing trails were not safe for automobiles. Railroads ran dangerously close to the old roads.

If engineers could link new and safer roads, it would work.

Again, Cyrus assured the other highway commissioners, **"I believe we can!"**

HOW ROADS WERE MADE

In the 1920's, roads were made from gravel, dirt, and crushed stone. Land had to be cleared and graded and then asphalt or concrete was added.

THE EARLY YEARS

Cyrus Avery was born on August 31, 1871 in Pennsylvania. He moved from Pennsylvania to Missouri with his family and later to Oklahoma.

AN ENTREPRENEUR

Avery was always solving problems.

1909. Avery built his farm.

1916. Avery built a span bridge over the Arkansas River.

1924. Avery created a gravity-pull water system from Spavinaw to Tulsa.

1928. Avery donated land for an airport.

Engineers explored all the trails and paths between Chicago and Los Angeles. They planned to weave roads together into one long, safe highway.

After two years, roads were connected but the work was still unfinished.

Without sign markers, travelers in their new cars took wrong turns, drove in circles, and got lost so engineers put finishing touches on the new highways with road signs, stop signs, and city markers.

"Make more shields with double sixes," Cyrus instructed the construction crews. Shields with the new numbers were installed just in time for the opening of the new road.

Cyrus beamed as he announced to the highway commissioner, "We connected the East to the West! The new road is safe and scenic."

Cyrus reported to the state governors, "We did it! Our highway is finished! We will call it Route 66 and it will open for traffic on November 11, 1926."

Dotted with businesses and landmarks, the new highway
shaped the landscape across the western United States.

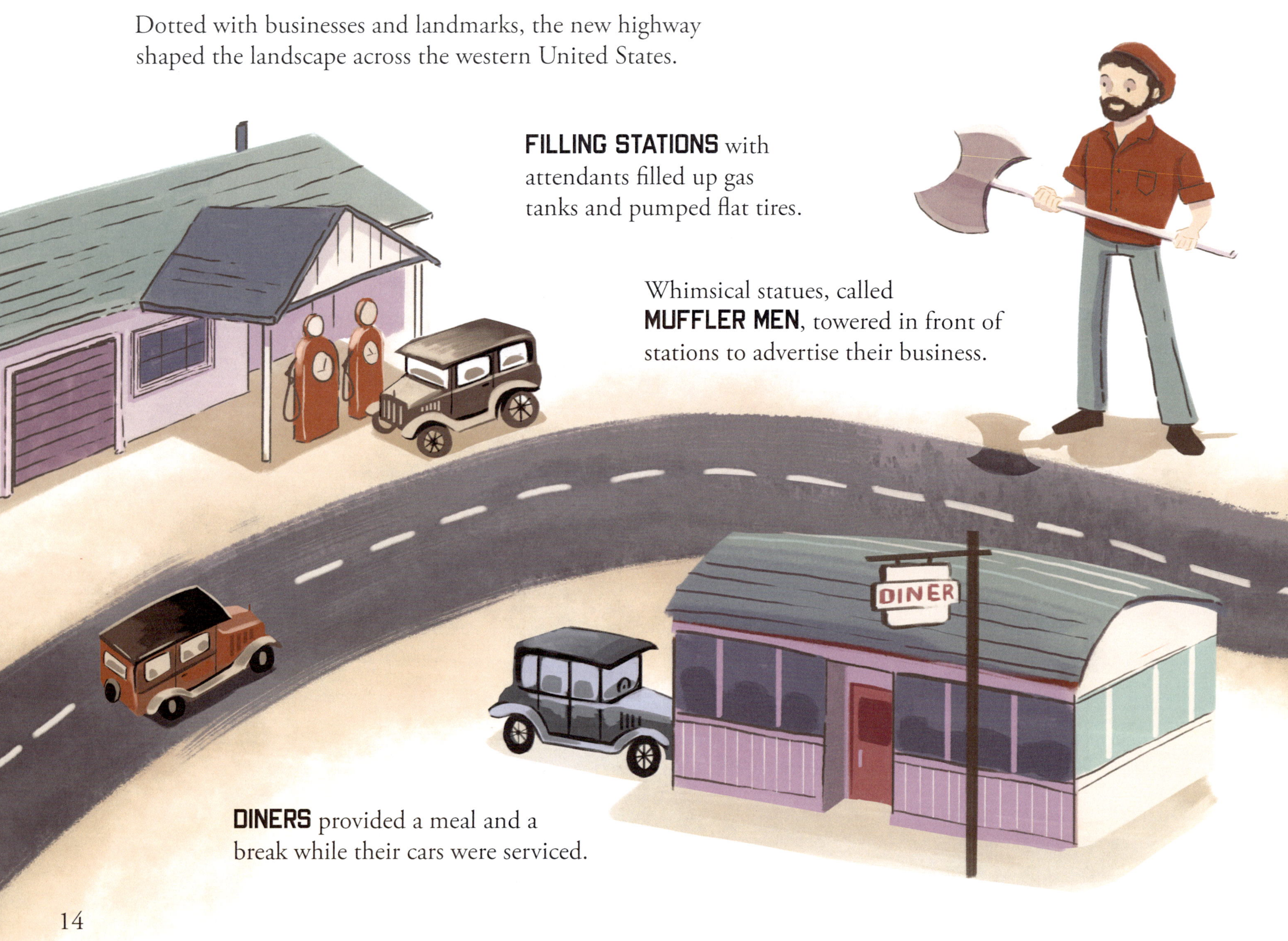

FILLING STATIONS with
attendants filled up gas
tanks and pumped flat tires.

Whimsical statues, called
MUFFLER MEN, towered in front of
stations to advertise their business.

DINERS provided a meal and a
break while their cars were serviced.

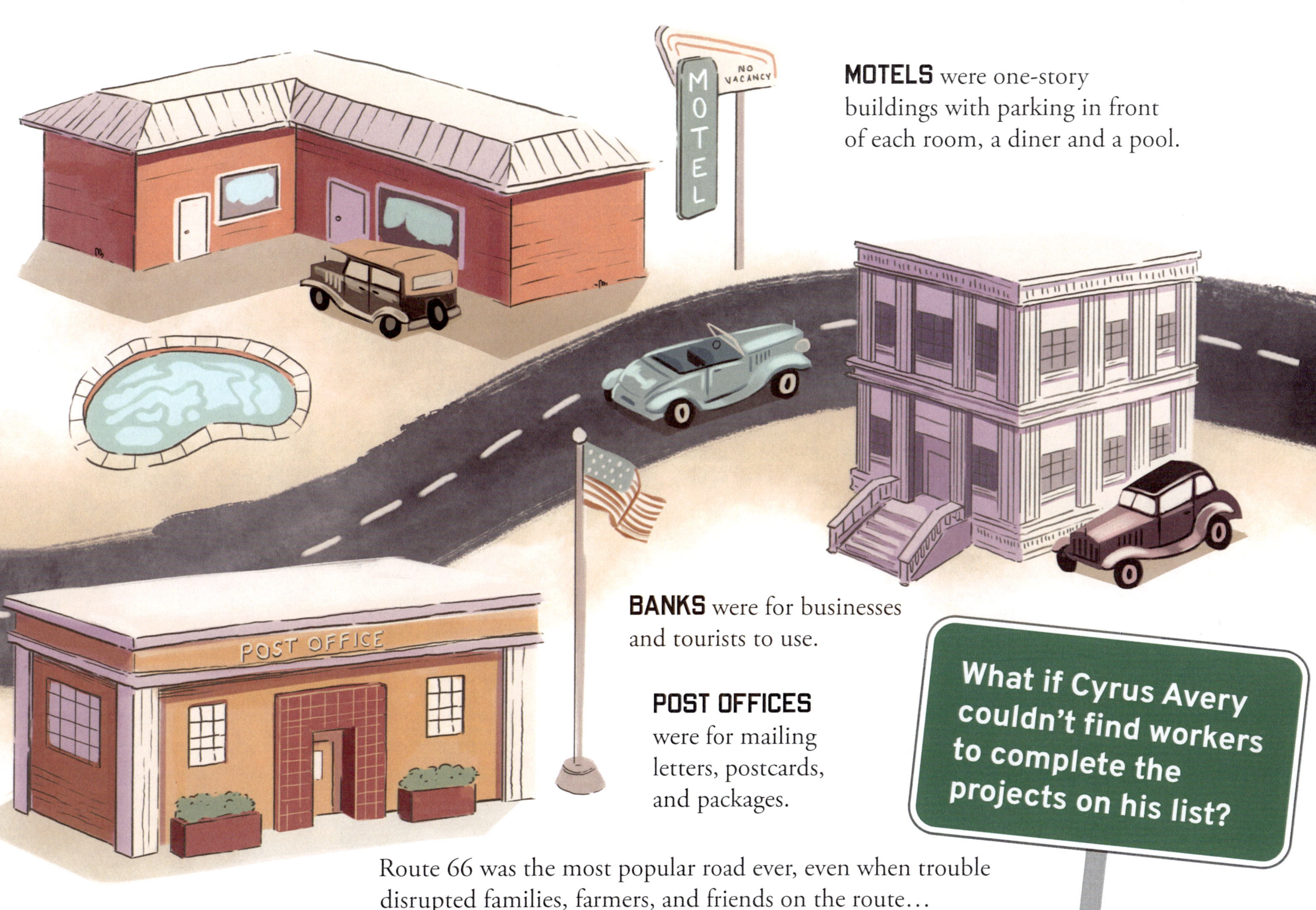

MOTELS were one-story buildings with parking in front of each room, a diner and a pool.

BANKS were for businesses and tourists to use.

POST OFFICES were for mailing letters, postcards, and packages.

Route 66 was the most popular road ever, even when trouble disrupted families, farmers, and friends on the route…

In the 1930's, a huge, dark cloud called a DUST BOWL blanketed many states in the middle of America. It destroyed homes, businesses, farms, and towns. Drought, high winds, and soil erosion devastated Oklahoma, Kansas, Texas, and New Mexico.

THE 1930s

The Dust Bowl, a time of dry and windy weather with devastating winds lasted from 1930-1936.

The black blizzard caused families to pack up and head west on Route 66.

There's the
Father of Route 66!
Hi, Mr. Avery!
Howdy, Cyrus!

By the 1940's, everyone knew Cyrus Avery and called him the "Father of Route 66".

Businesses continued to pop up everywhere along the new road and tourists from around the world came to see the magical highway. Cyrus, his team, and Route 66 had changed tourism in America.

THE 1940s

Cyrus is called The Father of Route 66.

WWII IMPACT ON ROUTE 66

The war (1941-1945) affected travel and business on Route 66. First, soldiers were at war and families stopped traveling. When they returned, there was a surge in traffic and business.

By the 1950's, every state on Route 66 showcased quirky landmarks that entertained tourists. Giant muffler men and women greeted tourists. A blue whale, a pink elephant, and rusty robots surprised everyone along the route.

In the desert, wildlife entertained all ages.

In the mountains, stargazers rushed to see night skies.

Route 66 was much more than a highway. It was the path America needed in times of trouble. Friendships were made from Chicago to Santa Monica. Festivals, car shows, and weekend celebrations brought families together year after year. Route 66, the uninterrupted highway, was busy twenty-four hours a day.

21

THE 1960s

Route 66 is no longer recognized as an official highway. The National Historic Preservation Act labels Route 66 an historic route.

FATHER OF ROUTE 66 DIES

Cyrus Avery died July 2, 1963 at the age of 91. In his final years, Cyrus continued to preserve the history of Route 66, support business owners, influence laws, and care deeply for tourism in America.

As Cyrus Avery grew older, so did Route 66. More automobiles, buses, motorcycles, vans, and shipping trucks were using the route than ever before. The winding highway that changed travel and tourism was crowded and in need of repairs. The highway was going to need a new advocate. Cyrus Avery was ready to retire and focus on his farm.

Once an oilman, farmer, and commissioner from a busy oil town, Cyrus changed how people travel. The Father of Route 66 taught others about exchanging ideas, making memories, and exploring new territories.

In 1985, the decommissioning of Route 66 was a serious problem for tourists and businesses. Route 66 was no longer considered an official highway. Decommission means to close a road, often leaving no one to care for it. Parts of the original route were now called state or scenic byways.

It was removed from the highway system and the maps but people who loved Route 66 stepped up to take care of the road.

In the 1990's, thanks to influencers and dedicated volunteers, Route 66 began a slow comeback as a cultural attraction. Tourists still traveled for friendship and entertainment just as they did in the 1920's and 30's. Route 66 was proving itself once again a popular destination for road and motorcycle trips. It offered a unique glimpse into America's past.

Today, people across America meet regularly to discuss ways to keep the route alive. New preservation laws and awareness along Route 66 promote the road and renew shops, gas stations, diners, landmarks, billboards, and motels.

THE 1990s

In 1990, Michael Wallis, author, historian, speaker, and Tulsan, wrote *Route 66, The Mother Road* to commemorate the history, people, places, and nostalgia of Route 66. His love of America's iconic road is a tribute to the people and places who influenced travel in America. Wallis published an updated, 75th Anniversary Edition in 2001. His passion for Route 66 and books is known around the world.

HELP IS ON THE WAY

- In 1985, Route 66 was designated as a National Historic Highway.

- Route 66 Associations promised to preserve highways in their states.

- The National Park Service started The National Route 66 Corridor Preservation Program promised to preserve resources.

- State-Level Legislation in individual states promised to preserve and promote programs to maintain landmarks, signage, and attractions.

- Federal and State Grants now support restoration and preservation and sometimes provide funding for projects that enhance Route 66.

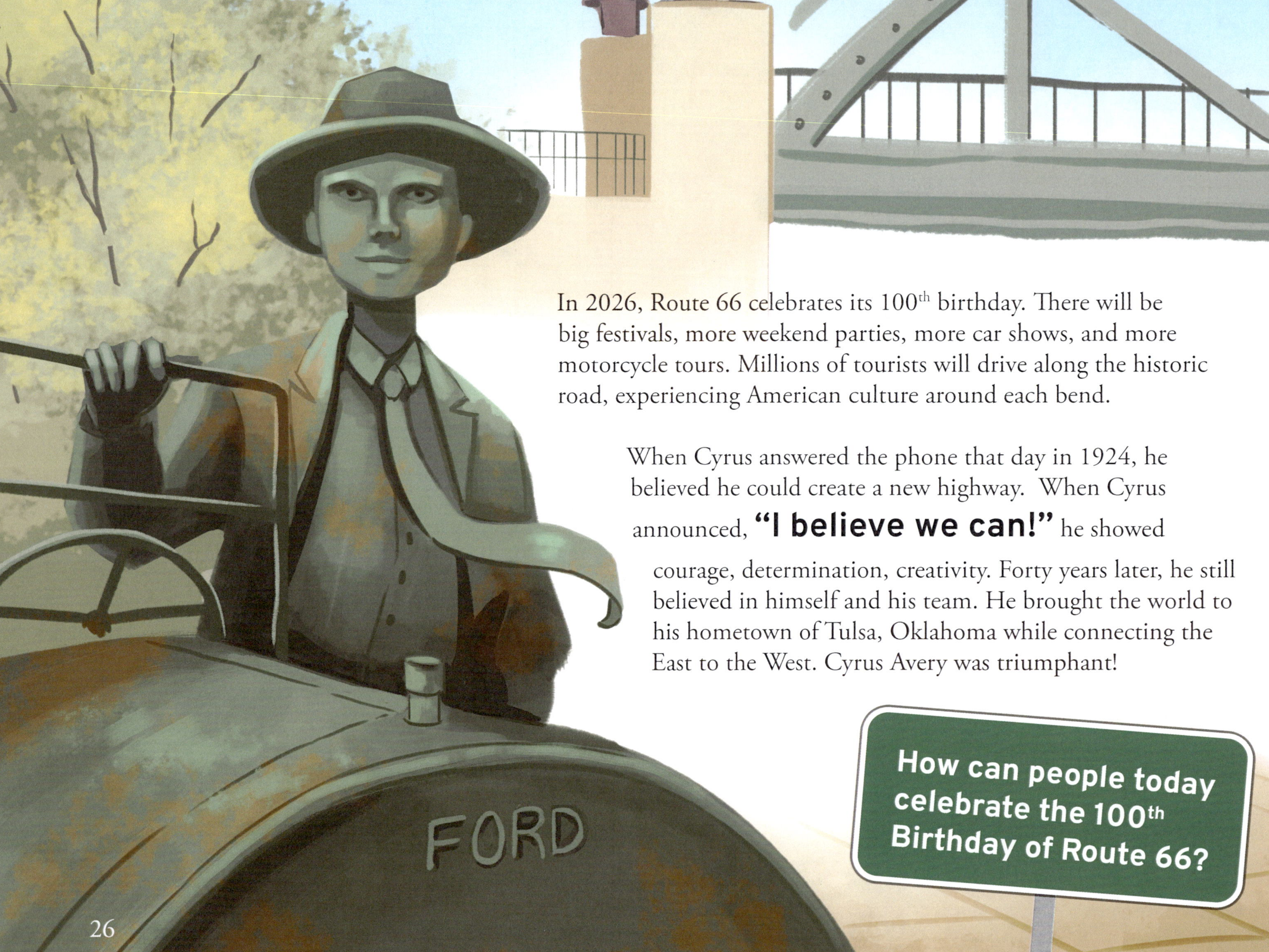

In 2026, Route 66 celebrates its 100th birthday. There will be big festivals, more weekend parties, more car shows, and more motorcycle tours. Millions of tourists will drive along the historic road, experiencing American culture around each bend.

When Cyrus answered the phone that day in 1924, he believed he could create a new highway. When Cyrus announced, **"I believe we can!"** he showed courage, determination, creativity. Forty years later, he still believed in himself and his team. He brought the world to his hometown of Tulsa, Oklahoma while connecting the East to the West. Cyrus Avery was triumphant!

ROUTE
66

CYRUS AVERY IS REMEMBERED

There are dozens of reminders of Cyrus Avery's contributions to travel in America:

Cyrus Avery Award established by The National Historic Route 66 Federation

Cyrus Avery Route 66 Memorial Bridge in Tulsa, Oklahoma

Tulsa Hall of Fame Inductee in 2004

Cyrus Stevens Avery Centennial Plaza located at Southwest Boulevard and Riverside in Tulsa.

Two books celebrating Route 66: Michael Wallis's "Route 66: The Mother Road, 75th Anniversary Edition"

Jim Hinkley's "The Route 66 Encyclopedia"

MAP OF ROUTE 66

GEMINI GIANT
LOU MITCHELL'S DINER
ILLINOIS
MISSOURI
MERAMEC CAVERNS
KANSAS
MILK BOTTLE GROCERY
THE GATEWAY ARCH
CADILLAC RANCH
OKLAHOMA
BLUE WHALE OF CATOOSA
TEXAS

GLOSSARY

Commissioner	a person in charge of a department or special job for the government
Decommission	when a road is no longer open to the public
Dust Bowl	a natural phenomenon with devastating winds, weeds, and dirt that destroys buildings and property
Festivals	a celebration of people gathering at a specific location for an event
Filling station	a service station for cars
Gravity pull system	underground system of pipes that takes liquid from one place to a lower elevation without a pump
Highway	a main road between towns or cities
Influencer	a person who works hard to persuade others about an idea or road
Motor court	a small hotel with parking in front of each room
Route	a road for traveling by walking or driving vehicles
Span bridge	a bridge with supporting arches that span across land or water
Stargazer	a person who studies astronomy and gazes at the night skies
Tourists	people who are out seeing places and things of interest

FUN FACTS

Who built the first wagon bridge across the Arkansas River?

Melville B Baird, a logger, J.D. Hagler, a merchant, and George Williamson, a banker paid for the bridge. The bridge opened to the public on January 4, 1904. Their courage showed how resilient Tulsans were. On top of the truss a small sign read, "You Said We Couldn't Do it, But We Did".

www.rhysfunk.com, 2018

Did Route 66 intersect the Trail of Tears?

Yes, it did! A portion of Route 66, from Rolla to Springfield, Missouri overlaps with part of the northern route of the Trails of Tears, where the US government forcibly removed the Cherokee Nation from their traditional homelands in the southern Appalachians to Indian Territory, now known as Oklahoma. 16,000 Cherokee traveled the Trail of Tears and an estimate 4,000 of them died along the way.

www.history.com/news/8-things-you-may-not-know-about-route-66, 8/30/2018

Who won the epic coast-to-coast foot race across America by running along Route 66?

In 1928, Andy Payne, a 20-year old Cherokee Nation citizen from Oklahoma, finished first in the 3,400-mile Bunion Derby that crossed America from New York to California.

When was Cyrus Avery born?

Cyrus Stevens Avery was born August 31, 1871 in Stevensville, Pennsylvania. When Cyrus was 14 years old his family moved to Indian Territory where they lived in a log cabin on Spavinaw Creek.

What were Cyrus Avery's hobbies?

As a child Cyrus loved to help his father on their farm in Pennsylvania. In 1908, as an adult, Cyrus bought a 1,400-acre farm in east Tulsa so he could have animals and crops. After he retired from his many jobs he continued studying plants and soil. He was fascinated by growing a variety of grasses and became a conservationist in the agriculture world.

Who wrote the song "Get Your Kicks on Route 66?"

Bobby Troup was a United States Marine from Pennsylvania who traveled on Route 66 after WWII. He was inspired to write the lyrics as he traveled Route 66. When he got to California, Troup met Nat King Cole, who soon recorded the song. Over 25 artists have recorded this song.

www.history.com/news/8-things-you-may-not-know-about-route-66, 8/30/2018

SELECTED SOURCES

ARTICLES

Avery, Ruth S. "Cyrus Stevens Avery" The Chronicles of Oklahoma 45. Spring 1967.

Corbett, William P.   "Oklahoma's Highways: Indian Trails to Urban Expressways" Ph.D. diss., Oklahoma State University. 1982.

Everett, Diana. "Avery, Cyrus Stevens" The Encyclopedia of Oklahoma History and Culture, https://www.okhistory.org/publications/enc/entry.php?entry=AV003.

Jones, James O. and Jones, Richard L. Tulsa, Okla.: Oklahoma Biographical Association. Oklahoma and the Mid-Continent Oil Field. 1930.

BLOG

Martin, Rhys. https://rhysfunk.com/2018/07/02/you-said-we-couldnt-do-it-but-we-did/

BOOKS

Bizzarri, Amy. The Best Hits on Route 66: 100 Essential Stops on the Mother Road. Rowman & Littlefield Publishing. December, 2018.

Everly-Douze, Susan. TULSA TIMES A Pictorial History: The Boom Years. World Publishing Co. 1987.

Hinkley, James. The Route 66 Encyclopedia. Voyageur Press. November 2012.

Lewis, Tom. Divided Highways, Building the Interstate Highways, Transforming American Life. Glass Frog Books. December, 2013.

McClanahan, Jerry. Route 66: EZ66 Guide for Travelers 4th Edition. National Historic Route 66 Federation, November 2019.

Scott, Quinta. Along Route 66. Norman, Oklahoma: University of Oklahoma Press, September, 2000.

Sonderman, Joe and Jim Ross. Route 66 in Oklahoma. Arcadia Publishing. December, 2011.

Wallis, Michael. Route 66: The Mother Road, 75th Anniversary Edition. St. Martin's Press, 1990.

Wallis, Michael, and Suzanne Wallis. Songdog Diary: 66 Stories from the Road. Tulsa, Oklahoma: Council Oak Books, 1996.

Zoellner, Tom. Traveling the New Route 66 Exploring America's Highways and the Stories They Tell. Counterpoint. October 2020.

COLLECTIONS

Photographs from Beryl D. Ford Collection at The Tulsa Historical Society

The Cyrus Avery Collection. http://osu-tulsa.okstate.edu/library/Father of Route 66 Timeline Final.htm. May 20, 2013.

GOVT DOC

Longfellow, Rickie. Federal Highway Administration. (2020) Back in Time. Route "66".   https://www.fhwa.dot.gov/infrastructure/back0303.cfm.

INTERNET

Dianna Everett. "Avery, Cyrus Stevens", The Encyclopedia of Oklahoma History and Culture. The Oklahoma Historical Society. https://okhistory.org/publications/enc/entry.php?entry=AV003

Nix, Elizabeth. The History Channel. https://www.history.com/news/8-things-you-may-not-know-about-route-66.

Route 66 in Oklahoma Historic Context Review. https://okhistory.org/research/forms/rt66/historiccontent.pdf. https://osu-tulsa.okstate.edu/library/Father%20of%20Route%2066%20Timeline%20Final.htm

PERSONAL INTERVIEWS

Avery, Marilyn Joy. Interview by Murray, Annette LaFortune. In-person interview. Tulsa, Okla. July 2019.

LaFortune, Robert J. Interview by Murray, Annette LaFortune. In-person interview. Tulsa, Okla. March 14, 2020.

MEDIA

Missouri State Libraries, April 4, 2017. Route 66 Oral History Collection (M67) with Marilyn Avery

NEWSPAPER

Krehbiel, R. (2016, October 29). "Meet the man who inspired Route 66". The Tulsa World Magazine. https://www.tulsaworld.com/entertainment/meet-the-man-who-inspired-route/article_abfd8374-e2bd- 5966-80f4-db7832b21dd6.html

YOUTUBE

Missouri State Library. April 4, 2017. Route 66 Oral History Collection with Marilyn Avery. Youtube.com/watch?v=If4pB3PuXZu&t=24s

City of Tulsa, Oklahoma. April 12, 2013. Route 66 Cyrus Avery Centennial Plaza, Tulsa's Route 66, Travels Towards Enhancement. Youtube/watch?v=3381Gg3Aq3U

Warren, Steve. Spavinaw Water-History Minutes. 2013. Youtube.com/watch?v=KYx16tU;D49

Lessing, J.W. December 12, 2013. Journey Down Rt. 66. Youtube.com/watch?v=KGGcAsJi44

CYRUS AVERY TIMELINE

1871	Cyrus Avery is born on August 31, 1871 in Stevensville, Pennsylvania.
1904	The wagon bridge is built across the Arkansas River between Tulsa and the new oil fields.
1916	The 11th Street Bridge, a two-lane bridge for pedestrians, will link travelers through Tulsa as they travel from Chicago to Santa Monica. This bridge is widened in 1935 to four lanes for vehicles.
1919	Cyrus Avery purchases land for the Avery Farm in Tulsa. He builds Avery Service Station, Old English Inn restaurant, and Avery Tourist Court, named "Avery Corner."
1921	Cyrus Avery is elected president of the Associated Highways Association of America.
1923	More than 15 million automobiles are registered in the United States. The Spavinaw Project begins. Cyrus Avery collaborated with local businesses to begin the 60-mile pipeline from Lake Spavinaw to Tulsa.
1934 - 37	Dust Bowl from drought and sandstorm sends thousands westward looking for new jobs and homes. Route 66 became the favored route to the west.
1937	Route 66 is paved from Illinois to California.
1963	Cyrus Avery passed away on July 2, 1963 at the age of 91.
2004	City of Tulsa renames the 11th Street Bridge, which carries Route 66 over the Arkansas River, the Cyrus Avery Route 66 Memorial Bridge.
2007	Dedication of the Cyrus Stevens Avery Centennial Plaza located at the site of the 11th Street Bridge in Tulsa.
2012	Dedication of East Meets West bronze sculpture of the Avery family in a 1926 Ford and horses pulling an oil field wagon. *Artist: Robert Summers. Foundry: Heart Foundry.*
2023	AAA Route 66 Roadfest begins as an interactive, family entertainment expo brings the route to people. A traveling exhibition that moves city to city.
2026	100th Birthday of Route 66. There will be hundreds of Centennial Celebrations planned across America to commemorate Route 66.

ROUTE 66 INFLUENCERS

Angel Delgadillo
SELIGMAN, ARIZONA

- Influenced Rt 66 State Associations in all 8 states by 1989
- Known as the "Guardian Angel of Route 66"
- Still operates family-owned business

Michael Wallis
TULSA, OKLAHOMA

- Historian and Author
- Route 66 Scholar
- Researcher
- Voice of the Sheriff in *Cars* (2006)

Jack & Gladys Cutberth
CLINTON, OKLAHOMA

Jack Cutberth

- Executive secretary of U.S. Highway 66 Association
- Known as "Mr. 66"

Gladys Cutberth

- Assisted Jack in running U.S. Highway 66 Association
- Donated memorabilia to Route 66 Museum in Clinton, OK

Annette LaFortune Murray is a lifetime traveler who lives on Route 66 in Tulsa, OK. She has been traveling the route since she was 5 years old. When she is not writing picture books, she is visiting libraries, playing pickleball, cooking at home, and dining out with friends. To learn more about Annette and her picture books, visit **www.annettemurraybooks.com**.

Bailey Vidler is a children's book illustrator from Phoenix, Arizona. She likes to go camping in Northern Arizona, exploring Route 66 with her border collie mix, Wyatt. To learn more about Bailey and her art, visit **baileyvidler.com**.